LOVE LETTERS TO YOUR MIND

NEHA RAUTELA

 pencil

ISBN 978-93-5667-496-7
© NEHA RAUTELA 2023
Published in India 2023 by Pencil

A brand of

One Point Six Technologies Pvt. Ltd.
123, Building J2, Shram Seva Premises,
Wadala Truck Terminal, Wadala (E)
Mumbai 400037, Maharashtra, INDIA
E connect@thepencilapp.com
W www.thepencilapp.com

Author biography

IS AN INTERNATIONALLY PUBLISHED POET, WRITER AND ARTIST.

CONTENTS

Acknowledgements

THANKING ALL MY FRIENDS FROM THE NEIGHBOURHOOD , THE MISFITS, THE ARTISTS, THE SEEKERS, THE ORIGINAL THINKERS

LETTER 01

01

DEAR DARLING

I hope that you are keeping well both physically and mentally.

Happy friendship day to you. Yes, you are my best friend!

Surprized, don't worry I'm not friendzoning you..

You know why most relationships fail after the initial chemistry fizzles off. It is because people do not communicate and understand each other well.

I want to understand you and kiss every scar on your soul….

I know that you have loved before, have had a family but still felt a strange emptiness, a numbness that did not stop following you.

Not that I'm commenting on your past for my own benefit but here I am you know, your sweet therapist who won't even charge a buck!

From what you told me about your ex, disappointment is natural

But it is okay to be disheartened in love. I have been cheated before. People were mean and selfish.

It gave me trust issues and what not.

But I know for sure you are not like them.

You were scared to love, you said I can find a "good boy"

!

I want you to know, that im done with the finding and consequent depression when my choices were not good enough

If god has made our paths to cross. It is for a purpose.

He has this plan chalked out for you and me.

So we have taken out the time and put in the efforts to help each other out.

Yes, we were supposed to meet like this.

Half happy, half sad….

You want to be loved. I want care and affection

So if someone is going to heal that heart of yours, let it be me.

Not that I will do your inner work. That you have to do yourself but I will be here to listen without judgement or any expectation.

I will always let you to just be.

I will be your friend first . I will value our relationship . you are not only my boyfriend but my mentor and my light.

Nothing works in one way.

You have been there for me these 2 years when I navigated through those tough memories. You picked up the pieces of myheart and helped me to trust someone again.

Yes, I trust you as much as I trust my own self and it is sucha liberating feeling.

You have never let me down.

You encourage me to follow my dreams.. you want me to find a scholarship abroad and pursue my interest and innate gift in art.

Really, no one ever took so much effort for me before you, not even my parents.

They thought im some machine which will give them ab output for the money they invested in my education.

I have enough bitterness when it comes to relationships but you are a sweet candy I want to taste.

Yes, I want to kiss yo on the lips. Tease your ears, give you a hickey on your neck. Kiss those lovely eyes and those dark circles underneath too.

I wonder when is the last time you slept properly without straining yourself. How many whiskey pegs in a day to forget the pain your last relationship gave you.

Trust me, escapism does not help anyone. REBOUNDS DON'T WORK . it is very rare to find someone who has the patience to help out their partner with issues ….

And about that thing of you not being a good man and me finding a better guy, lol.

I DON'T WANT TO FIND ANYONE. I have already received my share of sunshine and it is you!

My ex bf did not love me, it was just lust on his part. He did not care when I went to the cliff to die after breakup , infact he was the one who told me to die.

After such intense disappointment if I have had the courage to love again , you should too.

If life is giving me a chance and that is you, im all in.

 I always wanted a home and tried so hard to have a family of myown by being in a relationship . by getting married I thought I could find the care inherent in al homes.

But now I thank my stars that I am 31 and unmarried.

God saved me for you,

You care

You don't say it too often but your actions do.

You want the best for me,

The thought counts.

But guess what,

YOU ARE THE BEST FOR ME

WE ALL HAVE FLAWS
NO ONE IS PERFECTLY DESIGNED IN LIFE.
Its like a lock and a key.
You and I , we just fit.
This is one way of understanding it .
Destiny works in strange ways. Im glad things didn't work out for me before this, I deserved better;
I deserved someone who really cares .
I deserved a love as deep as the ocean itself and you, my sweetheart showed me such love exists beyond books and movies.
Oh. Yes
And having said that I know you work on every single thing to improve yourself.
It is the humbleness you have to recognize your flaws and mistakes, your sincere effort to be a better person everyday and the truth in your eyes
That I CHOSE YOU.
  I will select you over anyone anyday.
Remember we talked 24/7 for a month before you went in a no contact zone.
Time flew.
Einstein's eg of relativity seemed probable.
I wonder if its so great to talk to you and make love to you in my mind and how excited it makes me.
What would be the happiness quotient when we actually touch each other.
Oh and here I am kms away pining like an English poet of Victorian era for his lover
The first meeting,
The first kiss
The first sex

It keeps circling in my thoughts
The future belongs to you my baby
Because I am here with you
Just the two of us for eternity

LETTER 02

Hi babe,

You know sometimes when I think about you that song from delhi belly plays in my head-

I hate you

I love you

…..

Like seriously dude this is like mental bdsm.

You know like you hurt me and I'm still loving it

To some people this may seem apparently toxic but I know whatever you do has a reason and I trust your better judgement.

I tell you, perhaps its just that 30s are hard without sex or that I have played myself in bed with you like a million times by now; damn, you are so hot.

Like dunno why so hot and that piercing stare.

I love your eyes,

The way you gaze

So lost yet so profound

I love everything about you.

Everything I know and everything I am yet to know.

Darling, its like the words you use, the phrases they are fix in my head.

Gawd, I'm so obsessed with you.

Even if someone uses those words; there's a really cute smile on my face.

God! I miss you.
When will I get to hold you in my arms,
Make love to you
Undress your body
And when will you enter my flesh like you have entered
my soul.
I don't want you for a single night.
I want you everyday,
Every night
Just you and me,
Just US AND YOU KNOW WHEN ITS YOU I DON'T
HAVE A CARE IN THIS WORLD.
I KNOW, EVEN IF I MESS UP, YOU'RE HERE TO
PROTECT ME
BECAUSE I HAVE BEEN SO ALONE IN MY LIFE ,
you know its nice really liberating to not live under that
constant stress of having to worry about every little thing.
You got me covered
You wrap on me a blanket on cold winter mornings in my
dreams, sometimes you work as a blanket,
A brown sexy one
I WANT YOU, SKIN TO SKIN,
FLESH TO BONE,
RAW,
UNADULTERATED
WHEN YOU MAKE LOVE TO ME
I WANT YOU HERE
I WANT YOU NOW
I want to kiss your body, every part of it,
Every pore, every cut
I want to kiss away your sorrows

Anything bad you ever felt and I don't care what happens
to me in the process
Because my love for you is now beyond my control
Really there is no backing away now
No
Not FROM YOU
ALL MY THOUGHTS
MY WILDEST DESIRES
AND MY WEIRDEST FANTASIES ALL AWAIT
YOUR RETURN……

LETTER 03

Dear best friend

Sometimes I fail to understand you and your plans I get angry, I cry, but the very next day I put a brave face as if nothing ever happened. I don't know why things are so complicated .

I don't know what to feel

Do I feel anything at all

Sometimes I just go numb for days together

That same lurking emptiness of my soul howling and shrieking . I want to close the lids of my ears to all this noise.

I DON'T KNOW

WHY

WHEN

OR HOW I FELL IN LOVE WITH YOu

OR WHY I DO THE THINGS I DO FOR YOU

OR WHY LOVEIS SO FUCKING DUMB AND DEAF AND ALL YOUR REASONING GOES INTO YOUR KNEES AND ALL THE way out into the path through your toes

But inspite of all this breaking of old convictions and conditioning

I WANT TO BELIEVE YOU

I WANT TO TRUST YOU

I KNOW OURLOVE STORY is a bit odd, very different

from the common course of things in romantic relationships but honey
Look
I'M STILL HERE
AND ALTHOUGH YOU DON'T GIVE SOMEONE A CHANCE TO GO OR CHOOSE
YOU DID GAVE ME AN OPTION TO LEAVE LONG BACK
Maybe you didn't want to hurt me because you genuinely care
I have been hurt before
Who so ever I trusted with my feelings disappointed me
You know people lie
Show you Big DREAMS AND DON'T HAVE THE COURAGE TO WALK THE ROAD WITH YOU
BUT YOU ARE DIFFERENT
WE MAY SHOUT AT EACH OTHER
CRY OURSELVES TO SLEEP
BUT WE CRAWL BACK TO EACH OTHER
THAT'S HOW STRONG THIS IS
THAT IS HOW UNWILLING I AM TO LET YOU GO
YOU KNOW YOU HOLD THE KEYS to my heart
I thought I will not be able to feel anything after my break up in 2016
Like dude
My ex cried fake on many occasions
I mean I WAS SO COLD
I COULDN'T TRUST ANYONE
BUT THEN U
THAT HALF A TEAR IN YOUR EYES AFTER YOU READ MY POEM

THAT PICTURE OF YOU STANDING AND
STARING AT ME
YOU KNOW CHANGED MY MIND
I KNOWNOW FOR SURE
THAT I HAVE FOUND SOMETHING REAL

E ALTOGETHER

LETTER 04

DEAR BABY
I LOVE YOU
I MISS YOU EVERY MOMENT YOU ARE AWAY FROM ME
I MISS YOU
Every moment you are near, here in my thoughts
Infact my heart beats because
YOU ARE THE RHYTHM OF ALL ITS MUSIC.
I HAVE SURVIVED A LOT OF THINGS IN LIFE,
A traumatic childhood, a unloving family that constantly tried to bring you down, many heartbreaks and loss of a loved one
I KNOW WHAT PAIN SMELLS LIKE
OUR JOURNEY IS DIFFERENT AND YET IT IS SO SIMILAR
YOU ARE A MAN FIGHTING WITH HIS EMOTIONS
I AM A WOMAN FIGHTING WITH CIRCUMSTANCES
BUT WE ARE TOGETHER IN THIS
THAT'S ALL THAT MATTERS
I DON'T THINK WE MET BY SOME COINCIDENCE OR CHANCE
I KNOW I WAS CREATED IN GOOD THOUGHT BY GOD TO BE OF HELP TO YOU; to be by your

side; to be your forever friend and companion
 And to assist you in all your endeavours; wherever you want me to help you out.
YOU MAKE ME FEEL
YES, IT'S A A BIG DEAL
AFTER ALL THESE YEARS OF DESPAIR AND MEDICATION, YOU INFUSE IN MY VEINS THE POSSIBILITY OF BEING TRULY HAPPY IN LIFE. THE ASSURANCE OF PASSION, OF POWER AND A NEW LOVE WHERE I AM TRULY CARED FOR AND RESPECTED.
I really think before all this
I was in love with the idea of love and the wish to be loved in me was so strong but I was not loved back with the same intensity.

I was betrayed…over and over again
BUT WITH YOU
I DON'T FEEL INSECURE OR JEALOUS , MAYBE A LIL BIT BUT NOT MUCH
YOU FEEL DIFFERENT,
YOUR TOUCH FEELS DIFFERENT
YOUR WORDS CARESS THE INNER CORE OF MY CURIOUS SOUL
YOU, MY DEAR
YOU ARE SOMETHING ELS

LETTER 05

LETTER 05

DEAR baby
I DARE TO DREAM ABOUT A HOME AGAIN
LAST TIME MY DREAMS CAME CRASHING LIKE
A PACK OF CARDS
IT HURT BAD
I ALMOST DIED
BUT THANK GOD I DIDN'T
I didn't want to go through life without finding love
Thank God you happened,
Thank god I met you

LETTER 06

Letter 06

You are my first priority my one and only and really the
rest of the world doesn't matter
Most things that I do is an effort to please you
I want to make you happy, happier than ever,
Happiest infact!

YOU DESERVE IT
YOUR SOUL HAS SOUGHT THIS KIND OF LOVE
AND THAT IS WHY GOD MADE US MEET
YOU HAVE GIVEN ME EVERYTHING .
ALL THE THINGS THAT I THOUGHT EXISTED
ONLY IN ROMCOMS OR BESTSELLING NOVELS

FAITH, LOYALTY , TRUST AND COMPASSION

YOU LOVE ME MORE THAN I LOVE MYSELF
AND I LOVE MYSELF A LOT
YOU LOOK AT ME SMILINGLY AND MY DAY IS
MADE
I AM HAPPY TO BE ALIVE EVERYDAY BECAUSE
IT TOOK ME YEARS TO UNDERSTAND THAT
LIFE IS A GIFT

I WAS OKAY ALONE TOO
MAYBE EVEN GLAD I SIMPLY EXISTED
BUT YOUR COMING to my life has added that extra
zing to it!
The way you respond to my messages; the intricate nature
of yourcare;
The love you offer without asking for anything in return is
so soothing
I HAVE FELT BUTTERFLIES IN MY STOMACH
BEFORE BUT THIS IS DIFFERENT
YOU MAKE ME CALM

YOU'RE MORE LIKE AN ESSENTIAL OIL IN A
DIFFUSER THAT REDUCES ANXIETY ONLY BY
ITS PRESENCE IN MY ROOM
YOUR SMILE,
AHTHAT EFFERVESCENT ENERGETIC SMILE
THATFILLS M LIFE WITH WARMTH
YOU LOOK SOHAPPY WHEN YOU WORK
THE PASSION YOU have for your craft is so much ,
that it both inspiresme and attracts me to art even more!
The man who loves his work passionately /immensely
Also usually shows similar intense passion for their lover
You do everything perfectly in the sense that you give your
100% to something/ someone.
You RE EITHER IN IT, OR JUST NOT INTERESTED
ITS AN AMAZING QUALITY
YOU DON'T WASTE OTHER PERSON'S TIME
YOU SAY WHAT IS IN YOUR HEART
YOU KNOW THE DIFFERENCE BETWEEN LOVE
AND LUST
THERE ARE NO IN BETWEENS FOR YOU

YOU DON'T BREAK A PERSON'S HEART by fooling them into something that doesn't exist
You ask whatyou want straightaway
Your honesty in relationships appeal to me
And althoughi know everything about your past ,
All your flaws or lack of communicatin in your previous relationship ;
One thing is for sure

YOU, AS A PERSON ARE A VERY GOOD HUMAN BEING
TRUST ME, ONLY A GOOD HUMAN BEINGCAN BE A GOOD LOVER
BECAUSE LOVE IS SOMETHING WHICH EXPECTS ONE TO TRANSCEND ALL BORDERS OF SELFISHNESS AND BECOME ONE WITH ANOTHER PERSON.
A REAL LOVE AFFAIR MAY BE FEROCIOUS OR CALM BUT IT IS ALWAYS BETWEEN EQUALS
PEOPLE WHO ARE AT THE SAME LEVELOF MENTAL MATURITY, EMOTIONAL UNDERSTANDING AND SPIRITUAL CONSCIOUSNESS ….
WHEN SOMEONE HAS BASIC HUMAN VALUES LIKE KINDNESS, SELFLESSNESS AND THE LIKE THEY ARE FAR BETTER THAN ANY HONEY GILDED LIE
YOU KNOW I SEE SO MANY PEOPLE FAKING IT IN RELATIONSHIPS
SOME PEOPLE SHOW THEIR BEST part to a prospective partner especially when u talk of arrange marriages or people who meet on dating sites(not all cases

though)
But yes for that 3-4 month time inthebeginning its like a honeymoon phase.
Theyhide their secrets from one another and then try to be what their partner thinks they are and when they get married or start living together they find stark differences between expectations and reality
And then you see, this is where all the the drama starts-
THE UGLY FIGHTS, THE YOU SAID THIS BUT DAMN, 'I WAS SO WRONG TO BELIEVE IN YOU"
BUT LOOOK
OUR RELATIONSHIPIS SO DIFFERENT
DO YOU REMEMBER THAT IRFAN KHAN'S MOVIE QARIB QARIB SINGLE,LIKE YOU DID TAKE ME ON A WEIRD ADVENTUROUS JOURNEY.
WEIRD BECAUSE EVERYTIME I KNOW THINGS ABOUT YOUR PAST IT DOESN'T MAKE ME ANGRY INFACT I GIGGLE SOMETIMES AT HOW YOU WERE WITH THAT PARTICULAR PERSON ANDIT HURTS HOW THAT PERSON USED YOU BECAUE YOU WERE SO EMOTIONAL AND THOUGH PYAR KA PUNCHNAMA TAUGHT US NOT ALL GIRLS ARE GOOD;
YOU KNOW I DON'T REALLY JUDGE PEOPLE UNLESS I KNOW TOO MUCH ABOUT THEM WHICH IN YOUR CASE I KNOW INSIDE OUT WITH SURETY.
SOMETIMES YOU WERE THE ONE WHO WAS WRONG. YOU GOT SO BOTTLED UP INSIDE, YOU FORGOT HOW TO LOVE SOFTLY, YOU TOOK OUT THE FRUSTRATION OF A BAD

WOMAN ON A GOOD WOMAN..I UNDERSTAND THAT
BUTTHOSE WOMEN COULDN'T AND HENCE SOME HATED YOU
BUT ITS IMPORTANT FOR YOU TO GET THAT CLOSURE AND IM GLADMY GIFT OF EMPATHY HELPED IN IT.
I AM INTERESTED IN YOURPAST ONLY BECAUSE IM INTERESTED IN KNOWING YOU AND UNDERSTANDING YOU BETTER.
 Really I don't give a fuck about how many girls you slept with or what you did in a particular phase of your romantic life
Its okay
I UNDERSTAND LIFE, PEOPLE, SITUATIONS….
IM A POET AND I HAVE OBSERVED PEOPLE KEENLY SINCE CHILDHOOD AND TRIED TO ANALYSE THEIR BEHAVIOUS
WELL; thanks to my turbulent childhood I became an overthinker;
More vigilant about how society and people function
Now,
Surely you are SURPRIZED WHY I CALL MY UNHAPPY CHILDHOOD A BLESSING IN DISGUISE
SWEETHEART I HAVE LEARNT ONE THING in these terrific 31 years of my life
It is that there are always;
Always TWO ways of looking at a thing
Notice how TWO ppl react to a similar situation differently.
Like lord Buddha preached us

' no one can have power over you without your reaction'
The tough childhood taught me importance of a family;
Disappointment in love taughtme
Importance of love and care
And I think now,
In a highly materialistic world where you find educated rats
running faster than that cock in roadrunner cartoon show
Trying to cut each others throat
I know very acutely
THE IMPORTANCE OF A GOOD LOVING HOME
I APPRECIATE THE SILENCE OF A CHAOTIC
MOMENT.
I FLOW, LIKE A RIVER
I ALLOW ALL EXPERIENCES TO HELP ME GROW
INTO A BETTER PERSON; A MORE MATUREAND
OPEN MINDED VERSION OF ME
I WOULD NOT HAVE POURED MY HEART OUT
IN MY DIARIES FOR LIKE YEARS AND YEARS
BEFORE I WROTE MY FIRST POEM IF I HAD
SOMEONE TO SHARE MY FEELINGS WITH IN MY
HOME
SO THAT LONLINESS
THAT ALOOFNESS
AND THAT NEGLECT
GAVE ME THE STRONG DESIRE TO BE LOVED,
APPRECIATED AND UNDERSTOOD
I STUMBLED FIRST IN TRYING TO FIND A HOME
IN SOMEONE,
THE PAST DID HURT ,
THERE WERE SCARS ON MY SOUL
BUT YOU KNOW THE KINDNESS WITH WHICH
YOU TOUCH THEM AND MAKE THEM VANISH

MAKES MY EYES TEARY
YES I HAVE CRIED IN PAIN FOR LIKE MOST OF
MY CHILDHOOD And early youth but you make me cry
with happiness.
Really you do.....
BABY I LOVE YOU

LETTER 07

BABY I LOVE YOU

IM SO GLAD YOU ARE HERE ON THIS SAME
PLANET WITH ME.

YOU ARE HERE TO MAKE ME FEEL LOVED.
AND EVEN THOUGH I LEARNT THAT WE MUST
COMPLETE OURSELVES AND OUR HEALING,
YOU MY BABE
YOU WERE ALWAYS THERE.
YOU ANDI ARE FRIENDS FIRST
WE KNOW EACHOTHER'S ALL DIRTY SECRETS
AND INSTEAD OF JUDGING EACH OTHER-
WE LAUGH AND TEASE!
BECAUSE U GET ME LIKE NO ONE ELSE DOES
I DON'T KNOW HOW OR WHEN I BECAME SO
LUCKY THAT I FOUND SM1 WHO JUST FITS IN,
FITS IN WITH MYHOBBIES
WITH MY FLAWS AND QUALITIES
WITH MY FRIENDS AND FAMILY
AND WITH MY HOPES AND PLANS!
YOU KNOW THEY SAY MARRIAGES ARE MADE
IN HEAVEN.
I GUESS THEY ARE RIGHT.
GOD HAS A PLAN FOR EVERYBODY

I WONDER HOW DEATILED AND ACCURATE
THAT PLAN IS
I MEAN
Imagine meeting so many people in a lifetime
And yet MEETING SOMEONE ALL OF A SUDDEN
UNANNOUNCED;
HOPELESSLY   FASCINATED   BY   SOMEONE'S
CHARM AND INTELLIGENCE
THEY SAY IT TAKES A MOMENT TO FALL IN
LOVE
I THINK IN A MOMENT
ONLY ATTRACTION CAN HAPPEN
BUT WITH US
:
ITS SO FUCKING ELECTRIC,
I MEAN ITS LIKE MY VEINS ARE CARRYING A
BLOOD TYPE-U
LOL
JOKES APART
THIS KIND OF LOVE FEELS FRESH EVEN AFTER
ALL THESE YEARS
I MEAN;
I WAS FASCINATED BY YOU
IN THE FIRST CONVERSATION ITSELF;
BUT YOU AND I ;
AS WE HAVE COME TO KNOW EACH OTHER
BETTER
ARE AGING LIKE FINE WINE IN THIS
RELATIONSHIP
YOUKNOW I LOOK FORWARD TO EVERY NEW
DAY WITH MORE ENTHUSIASM NOW
YOU HAVE NO IDEA HOW MANY TIMES I HAVE

ZOOMED YOUR PICS IN MY PHONE AND KISSED YOU
HOW MANY TIMES I IMAGINEYOU TOUCHING ME
KISSING MY FACE;
THEN MY LIPS
AND THEN MY ENTIRE BODY.
THE VERT THOUGHT OF YOU AND ME IN BED,

MAKES ME THINK FLASHES OF 50 SHADES OF GREY IN MY HEAD
LO BEHOLD
FROM WHAT I KNOW ABOUT YOU TILL NOW I KNOW YOU ARE MUCH MORE CREATIVE AND EXPERIMENTATIVE THAN MR. GREY
YOU LOOK FOR NEW EXPERIENCES,
HEY,
ME TOO
I THOUGHT IT WAS QUITE A PROBLEM UNTIL I MET YOU
NOW YOU AND I
CAN TRAVEL THE WHOLE WORLD WITH CHILDLIKE CURIOSITY'
AND ENJOY EVERY SINGLE DAY
I ALWAYS THOUGHT A 9-5 JOB KINDA GUY WOULD BE BORING FOR ME
BECAUSE I SEEK CONSTANT ADVENTURE
AND THOUGH IM SUCH A SUCKER FOR A STABLE ROMANTIC RELATIONSHIP
I WILL DO EVERYTHING IN MY POWER TO SPICEUP OUR RELATIONSHIP.

BETWEENME AND YOU;
A DULL MAN WOULD HAVE BORED ME TO DEATH
THANK GOD , You are NOT BORING INFACT UR FAR FROM BORING
LIKE AN ONION,
ONE   PEEL   AFTER   ANOTHER   I   LOVE DISCOVERING the inner you.
I LOVE YOU BABE
EVERYPART OF U

LETTER 08

I LOVE YOU BABE
EVERY PART OF U
DON'T THINK ANY TRUTH ABOUT YOU WOULD
MAKE ME LOVE YOU ANY LESS....
INFACT BETWEEN US WHAT WE KNOW ABOUT
EACH OTHER ITS LIKE BIRTHING A NEW
SAPLING FROM A SEED THAT IS GROWING IN
THE MIDDLE OF A CONCRETE PATH
THE PLANT IS BLOOMING NOW AND SOON
THERE WILL BE FRUITS IN IT
THE ROOTS OF THIS PLANT IS MUTUAL
UNDERSTANDING , APPRECIATION FOR LIFE
AND AN UNFLINCHING SENSE OF DEVOTION
THAT MY LOVE,
IT IS RARE
AND BOTH U AND I KNOW THE VALUE OF IT
THAT IS WHYU TREASURE ME SO MUCH AND I
TREASURE YOU TOO !one day with you is like a bliss
Remember that pirates of the Caribbean hero-heroine
scene but gawd, no haaan
I want u with me
Every single day
I want to see you sleep in my arms
I want to kiss your forehead and eyes everyday
I want to pray for you and with you

I want to inspire you to take chances and give you all the moral support you need to put the past in the past.
BECAUSE BABE I TELL YOU TO BE STRONG BUT THE VERYNEXT MOMENT I REALISE YOU CARRY the WEIGHT OF THE WORLD ON YOUR SHOULDERS,
YOU STURDY RATHER SEXYSHOULDERS
FORGIVE MY THARAK
ITS THAT TIME OF THE MONTH AND IM SUDDENLY FEELINGALL HORMONAL LOL
SO MY POINT WAS YOU ARE STRONG
LIKE MENTALLY U R VERY STRONG
STRONGER THAN ANYONE I KNOW
IT ISJUST THAT YOU DID NOT FIND ANYONEWHO COULD BEAR THE BURDEN OF THAT STRENGTH WITH YOU
WHO COULD BE PATIENT ENOUGH WITH YOU
WHO COULD LOVE YOU WITH A GREATER INTENSITY THAN THE STRENGTH OF YOUR DOUBTS AND INSECURITIES !
YOU WERE NOT MEANT FOR AN AVERAGE LOVE,
AND DEFINITELY NOT AN AVERAGE LOVER
PEOPLE YOU LOVED WERENOT NECESSARILY BADPEOPLE BUT THEY WERENOT WHAT YOUDESERVED
ITS JUST THAT U HAVE STRUGGLED SO MUCH ALONETHAT IT MADE U KINDOF RETICENT
AND LIKE MR. DARCY PPL TOOK YOUR PAIN FOR YOUR PRIDE
No u Are not proud

You've just been hurt in romantic relationships before
and it has caused u such torment in the past that u felt
numb
Know that all feelings are valid even numbness
It doesn't make u any less of a person
Infact itindicates that u feel toomuch with a deeper
intensity

LETTER 09

Than most people
 I have felt sadness for decades
Before I met u
So I know what depression loneliness can be like
Though not as intense as ur experiences
My emphatetic nature gives me a sneak peakinto ur emotions and overall sense of being....
U knowlike a dark scary cave
U can drive away someone who is afraid of facing trouble or challenges for a loved one
Adveristy
is truly the test of all relationships
MOST PEOPLE THINK A RELATIONSHIP IS LIKE AN ICE CREAM AND THEY ONLY WANT TO LICK THE SWEET PART
BUT THEREAL TEST OFRELATIONSHIP COMESIN BAD TIMES
 And now that we have faced this one bad year together we know for sure that we as a team can survive anything and trust me babe,
When I'm saying this
THAT WHEN IT COMES TOU,
I AM CAPABLE OF ANYTHING
I AM NOT SAYING THIS FOR THE SAKE OF JUST SAYING THIS

BUT ON SEVERAL OCCASIONS I HAVE PROVED
TO YOU I WILL NEVER LEAVE UR HAND
THAT I AM HERE 2 STAY
THAT I AM YOURS FOREVER
AND TRUST ME BABE
TRUST ONELASTTIME
A UNDESERVING MORTAL
I WILL NEVER EVER LET U DOWN
UR FAITH INME WILL NEVER MEET THEFACE
OF SHAME
IN ALL LIFETIMES
ONLY U WILL BE MY PRIORITY

I don't know when I will get to marry you; though it will
be the best day of my life.
I want to be officially yours .
I hope that day comes soon when I get to add your
surname next to mine.
I wish; I sincerely hope with all my heart, you take me
soon to our home where you and I can live.
I just want to lie next to you; whisper sweet nothings in
your ears;
Tease your ear lobe, lick it and keep kissing every part of
your bare body all night.

LETTER10

Dear sweety,

Now mom is telling me to get married soon. Urgh,, I wish you could come back in a few months. I want to marry you.

I cannot imagine spending a single night with someone else, let alone whole life and you know marriage should be done for love and not circumstances or money or anything else for that matter.

I want only you to touch my body.

 only you are always in my thoughts

I love you

I want you

A 1000 times yes,

Only you!

You can light me up after a hard day. I don't know when or where or how I started loving you so much and this time I feel so positive and strongly about love.

YOUR ADDITION IN MY LIFE HS SUBSTRACTED ALL SORROWS. YOU HOLD MY HAND, EACH STEP OF THE HEALING PROCESS.

MY EX BOYFRIEND OR LOSS OF LOVED ONE,any memory that otherwise makes me wince in pain.

You being here with me , gives me the courage to look back at those happy or sad memories.

You are MY ROCK,
AND NO MATTER HOW MUCG THE WORLD
MADE ME CRASH, I AM GLAD I FINALLY
LANDED AT YOUR SHORE.
TOGETHER, WE WILL ONLY MAKE BLISSFUL
SOUNDS.
I don't know anything about my soul. Some tarot reader
say im new, some mystics say im really an old soul.
Lol
Dunno and now it kind of doesn't really matter.
If I have met you FOR THE FIRST TIME OR YOU
HAVE BEN MY PARTNER IN PREVIOUS LIVES.
WHAT REALLY MATTERS IS THAT IN THE HERE
AND NOW, I LOVE YOU TO BITS AND PIECES.
YPUR SMILE, YOUR VOICE , YOUR GAZE,
EVERYTHING IS ATTRACTIVE.
BUT MORE FASCINATING IS YOUR SOUL.
YOUR YEARNING FOR SOMETHING REAL.
SOMETHING THAT CAN MAKE YOU FEEL ALIVE
WHEN YOU ARE SURROUNDED BY THE
GHOSTS OF YOUR PAST.
I KNOW YOU HAVE A PAST.
I HAD A PAST TOO.
BUT MINE HURTS VERY LITTLE NOW AND I
HOPE, OH GOD , I SINCERELY HOPE
THAT THESE TWO YEARS HAVE HELPED YOU
FEEL.
 I KNOW YOU HAVE EXPERIENCED LOSS OVER
AND OVER AGAIN
Like your soul is as old as it gets.
No sorry im not being mean about it but you have been
here for quite a long time now.

You have seen people come and go,
Creation, destruction, magic,miracles, good , bad, water and flame, nothing and everything!
Your soul as im told by you has been through so much that it had stopped feeling and now this sudden upsurge of emotions for you in a young girl who is simply enamored by your mere existence.
WHO LIVES EVERYDAY IN HOPE OF MEETING YOU SOMEDAY,
WHO LOVES YOU
MORE THAN SHE LOVES HERSELF;
IS CERTAINLY OVERWHELMING FOR YOU AND I UNDERSTAND THAT.
ITS OKAY BABE,
PERHAPS, LOVE marriage and kids have been a repeated drama.
Perhaps a partner dying has been a repeated drama
Like an endless loop devoiding you of all emotion!
Or seeing your whole world crash right in front of your mystic eyes has caused you unspeakable trauma.
YET YOUR SOUL CHOSE LOVE ALWAYS!
IN HOPE THAT YOUR PARTNER WON'T CHOOSE DEATH OVER YOUR LOVE, IN HOPE THAT THE LOOP OF EMOTIONAL DEVASTATION WILL ONE DAY BREAK AND PERHAPS YOU CAME DOWN TO EARTH IN SEARCH OF HER;
BUT MET ME INSTEAD.
SO MEETING ME MUST HAVE DAZZLED YOU.
NOT THAT IM UGLY, IM VERY BEAUTIFUL AS I AM TOLD BY COUNTLESS MEN AND EVEN WOMEN.
BUT im speaking from a emotional point of view

Meeting sad and depressed and lonely people must have been your thing because you related most to despondent feelings but to see this undying enthusiasm , this infallible hope in me
That urge to always live and succeed at everything I do
This precisely , in my opinion made you take a second glance at me.
 OBVIOUSLY , YOU HAVE THE KIND OF MONEY THAT CAN MAKE ANY GIRL SAY YES TO YOU AND I KNOW, IN TODAY'S WORLD LOVE IS CHEAP AND EASY.
MOST PEOPLE ARE SO MATERIALISTIC.
I mean if someone makes an id on a matrimonial site the first thing a woman's asks a man is his salary
Whether he has a house of his own
And if he would live with his parents after marriage!
To think of it,
People want to break homes even before officially being a member of it.
People have become so insensitive to human pain and myriad other emotions.
They just want things fast in this modern world.
But I have ALWAYS THOUGHT DIFFERENTLY, MAYBE BECAUSE I DIDN'T GET THE LOVE OF A FAMILY WHEN I WAS A CHILD.
WHATEVER BE THE REASON
MY SOUL KNOWS HOW IMPORTANT it is to have a family, someone who really cares and GOD HAS TAUGHT ME THE VALUE OF FAMILY AND LOVE BOTH; THE HARD WAY OFCOURSE!
YOU MAY NOT FORGET HER.
IM NOT HERE TO TAKE SOMEONE'S PLACE

IM HERE TO MAKE YOU HAPPY
I JUST WANT THE BEST FOR YOU.
AND I AM THE BEST FOR YOU!
 TRUST ME
THROUGH ALL THESE UPS AND DOWNS,
KNOWING YOU INSIDE OUT, HATING AND
LOVING YOU
EVERYTHING WE HAVE BEEN THROUGH IN
THIS RATHER RICKETY JOURNEY
ONE THING IS FOR SURE
WE ARE HERE TO STAY!
WE,
ARE A NEW FOREVER!
IT IS BOTH A BOON AND A BANE TO LOVE
SOMEONE SO MUCH.
SO MUCHSO, THAT NO OTHER LOVE WOULD
SUFFICE
I DREAM OF YOU
IN MY DREAM I AM SEEING YOU CLOSE TO
MW,SOMETIMES JUST LISTENING TO YOUR
VOICE AND SEEING YOUR PHOTOS.
THE MIND HAS AN amazing mechanism.
What is hard in real at the moment is easy and natural in
the dreamscape.
And interestingly I am not doing things to you in my
dream,
NO KISSES NO SEX
NOT EVEN HOLDING HANDS
I JUST SEE YOU SIMPLY and OH! THE JOY IT
GIVES TO MY YEARNING HEART! WHICH IS JUST
TOO ENGROSSED IN THE THOUGHTS OF YOU
LIKE IM SLEEPING OR WAKING I AM THINKING

OF YOU.
DAMN, this obsession its both thrilling and scary.
WHAT IF YOU LEAVE?
WHAT IF YOU DON'T FEEL EXACTLY HOW I
FEEL!
THOUGHTS CROSS MY MIND
AND MAKE ME NERVOUS.
BUT THEN
I CHOOSE TO HOPE,
LIKE I ALWAYS HAVE.
CHOOSE TO THINK ONE DAY YOU WILL HOLD
ME IN YOUR ARMS AND NEVER LET ME GO….